THE SIX FOOLS

COLLECTED BY

ZORA NEALE HURSTON

ADAPTED BY **Joyce Carol Thomas**

ILLUSTRATED BY **Ann Tanksley**

HARPERCOLLINS*PUBLISHERS*

A dashing young man courted a pretty young woman. After they had dated a long, long time, he asked her to marry him.

"Yes," she answered sweetly.

So as was the custom, the young man sat down with her mother and father and discussed his intentions.

Her parents were very glad, for he was strong and worked hard. He saved his money and therefore could provide well for their daughter and the children they would have.

The father said, "Yes, young man, my wife will plan a nice wedding."

The mother said, "Daughter, go to the cellar and draw a cold pitcher of the sparkling cider. Let's celebrate and make merry!"

The happy daughter took the pitcher and went down to the cellar. She turned the spigot, and the refreshing golden cider gushed into the jug.

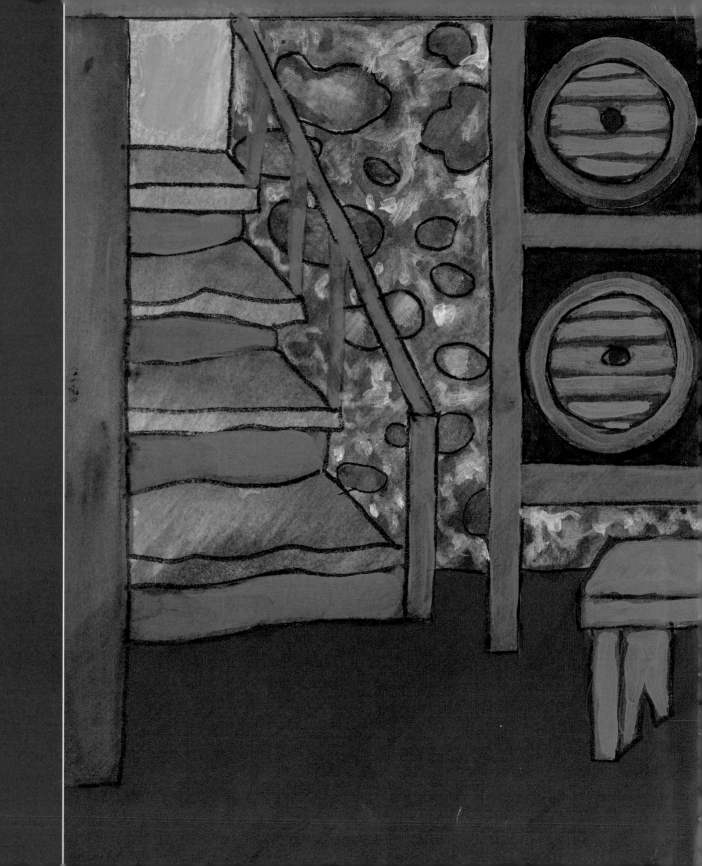

While the sparkling cider was running, she started daydreaming, thinking that after she and the young man got married and had a child—what would she name it?

She sat and thought and thought and the bubbling cider ran and ran.

The thirsty young man waited patiently for his cool drink. After a long time the mother said to the father, "What can be keeping our daughter?"

So she went down to the cellar to see what was the matter.

"What's taking you so long to come back with the apple cider, Daughter?"

The daughter said, "Mama, I just got to thinking. When we get married and have a baby, what will we call it?"

The mother knitted her brow. "Daughter, that *is* something to think about."

So the mother sat down beside her daughter and began to think, too. The bubbling cider was still running.

They thought and thought, and after a long time, the father excused himself from the patient young man and went down to see what was the matter.

"Wife! What are you doing letting all our good cider go to waste?" The father worked hard, saved, and didn't waste his money. "Why, I'll be ruined! Remember our daughter hasn't even married the young man yet."

"Well," said the mother, "we've just been wondering what to name the baby after she and the young man marry and have a child."

The father said, "Now that *is* something to study about. Why, I never gave it a thought."

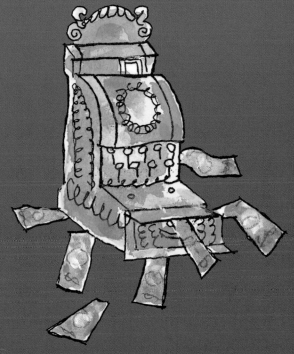

So the father sat down and
began to daydream, too.

Way after while, the young man got more
thirsty and went to see what was holding up his drink.

"What are all of you doing sitting down here in a flood of apple cider?"

The father said, "We're just studying what to name your firstborn after
you and our daughter get married and have a baby."

"Well," said the young man, "you are the three biggest fools that I ever laid eyes on. I'm going traveling for a year, and if I find three fools as big as you, I'll come back and we'll get married."

He traveled and traveled,
and way after while he saw
a man leaping up in the air
by a bush with some clothes
on it. The man just kept
jumping up in the air and
falling back.

"What are you doing?" the young man asked.

The jumping man said, "Those are my trousers on that bush and I'm trying to get into them."

The young man said, "Well, why don't you take them in your hands and pull them on?"

"I never thought of that," said the jumping man. Then he took them in his hands and pulled them on.

"That's *one* fool," said the young man, and traveled on.

He saw a farmer trying to
raise a cow up on the roof
of a barn by a rope around
her neck. He pulled and
pulled, but he could not lift
the cow up on the barn.

"Just what are you trying to do?" asked the young man.

The farmer pointed up to the roof of the barn. "See all that grass growing on top of the barn? I'm trying to pull the cow up there so she can eat."

"Why don't you toss it down to her?" asked the young man.

"Oh, I never thought of that," said the farmer.

"Now that makes *two* fools," the young man said, and traveled on.

One day the young man
saw a woman rushing in
and out of her house,
pushing a wheelbarrow.
She had placed a wide
board at the door like a
gangplank and kept dashing
in and out, in and out with
the wheelbarrow.

The young man said, "What are you moving
in that wheelbarrow? I can't see anything in it."
"Oh," she said, "I have scoured my kitchen,
and I'm trying to haul in some sunshine to dry it."
He said, "Why don't you open the doors and
windows and let the air dry it for you?"
"Oh! I never thought of that."

"Well, well, w-e-l-l," said the young man, "I have found *three* folks as foolish as the *three* fools I left. So I might as well go back and get married."

By that time I left.

ADAPTER'S NOTE

In Zora Neale Hurston's *The Six Fools* we sit with our feet bubbling wet as we stand ankle-deep in a cellar flooded with apple cider.

Next we're in a backyard, leaping with a man hoping to land in his pants hanging on a bush. Even though he keeps missing, he keeps jumping. Odd?

We are the woman trying to wheelbarrow sunshine into the scrubbed house. We go back and forth, in and out, again and again. Astonishing?

We are the farmer working to lift the hungry cow *by a rope* to the top of a barn so she can eat the grass sprouting there. We pull hard on the rope, repeating his failure. Outlandish?

Is it human nature to make fun of the foolishness of others, even as you and I also chuckle about the mistakes we continue to make? We are the only beings on this planet who can laugh until we ache at the impossible and the incredible.

Know what? I think I'll read *The Six Fools* again. And sparkle with Zora Neale Hurston's laughter as golden as bubbling apple cider.

—JOYCE CAROL THOMAS

ARTIST'S NOTE

I was introduced to Zora Neale Hurston in 1988 when her book *Their Eyes Were Watching God* mysteriously appeared on my doorstep. I began reading the book immediately and was completely enthralled with her work.

One week later I began my first interpretive painting based on a scene from *Their Eyes Were Watching God.*

Zora has given me many hours of enjoyment. Her imagination has stimulated my creativity. I am a better artist for having met her.

—ANN TANKSLEY

JUMP AT DE SUN

To my nephew, Tyler, with love
—J.C.T.

To my husband, John,
and my grandchildren,
Jillian and Donnie Rice
—A.T.

The Zora Neale Hurston Trust gratefully thanks Ann Tanksley for her superb work. The Trust is also very thankful for the vision and guidance of Susan Katz, Kate Jackson, and our wonderful editor, Phoebe Yeh. Lastly, our continued appreciation of Cathy Hemming, who initially brought us to HarperCollins Children's Books, and Jane Friedman and everyone at HarperCollins who works tirelessly on behalf of Zora.

Source as it appeared in *Every Tongue Got to Confess: Negro Folk-Tales from the Gulf States*: Hattie Reeves, born on Island of Grand Command, West Indies; about 50; domestic.

On page 35, Zora Neale Hurston delights us by using a Caribbean-flavored expression: "By that time I left" means "The End." —J.C.T.

The Six Fools   Text copyright © 2006 by Zora Neale Hurston Trust
Adapter's copyright © 2006 by Joyce Carol Thomas   Illustrations copyright © 2006 by Ann Tanksley
Manufactured in China.   All rights reserved.   www.harperchildrens.com
Library of Congress Cataloging-in-Publication Data
Thomas, Joyce Carol.
The six fools / collected by Zora Neale Hurston ; adapted by Joyce Carol Thomas ;
illustrated by Ann Tanksley.— 1st ed.   p.   cm.   Adapted from a story collected by Zora Neale Hurston
and previously published in Every Tongue Got to Confess.
Summary: A young man searches for three people more foolish than his fiancée and her parents.
ISBN 0-06-000646-3 — ISBN 0-06-000647-1 (lib. bdg.) [1. African Americans—Folklore.
2. Folklore—United States.] I. Tanksley, Ann, ill. II. Hurston, Zora Neale. Six fools. III. Title.
PZ8.1.T3765Six 2005   2004030055   398.2'089'96073—dc22

Typography by Carla Weise 1 2 3 4 5 6 7 8 9 10 ❖   First Edition